FLIPPIN' OUT

REAL ESTATE RESCUE COZY MYSTERIES, BOOK 1

PATTI BENNING

SUMMER PRESCOTT BOOKS PUBLISHING

CHAPTER ONE

Flora Abner wasn't having a good day. Scratch that, she wasn't having a good month. No, she wasn't having a good *year.* When did things go so wrong?

She was tempted to say it had started with Kyle, because her good for nothing, gold-digging, cheating boyfriend had certainly been the lowlight of her year so far, but blaming him was a little too easy. In truth, her life had started on its downward spiral ten years ago, when she had declared her accounting major. She … hated accounting. She had always hated accounting, but at the time it had seemed like a smart, reasonable decision. Accounting paid decently, there were plenty of jobs, and it would help prepare her for one day becoming more involved in her family's business, if she wanted to. It had felt, at the time, like the responsible choice.

But the problem with choosing a major in something she hated was that it had landed her a job she … well, she couldn't quite say she hated it. Her coworkers were nice, her boss was decent, and she had plenty of stability. But the thought of doing it for the rest of her working life had started filling her with an existential, soul-sucking dread just a couple of years in, and that feeling had only gotten worse with time.

So, the current state of her life was probably mostly thanks to that one, fateful decision when she was nineteen, but Kyle Groener was a close second, and he was the reason she had spent most of her weekend hiding in her apartment, feeling bad for herself.

"I can't believe I wasted four years of my life with him." She sniffed and pulled Amaretto, her fluffy white Persian cat, closer to her chest. Her own dark blonde hair fell over the cat's face, making her whiskers twitch. "I'm done with dating. I'm going to be a spinster with five cats and more houseplants than I can count."

At least houseplants wouldn't cheat on her. The

cats, however, would probably throw her to the wolves for a can of tuna. That was okay. Cats were cute enough that she could forgive them for almost anything.

Amaretto tolerated the forced cuddle for a few moments, then squirmed free and jumped from the couch to the coffee table, where she licked the fluffy fur on her shoulder and gave Flora an offended look, her yellow eyes full of judgment.

"Everyone leaves me, even you," Flora moaned, turning over to stare at the ceiling.

She knew she was being dramatic, but she deserved this weekend of misery. She still felt a little bad for backing out of the family dinner on Friday, but come tomorrow morning, she would need to shove all of this misery down and lock it in a box so she could pretend everything was all right at work. A part of her was tipping on the edge of doing something drastic like quitting, but she needed the money. The Abners might be well off, but her parents were clear on their expectations. She and her siblings had to earn their own way and support themselves. Her parents would chip in in a true emergency, but she knew quitting her job with no backup plan because she was depressed and sad wouldn't count.

Amaretto flopped down on the coffee table, her plush tail dangling off the edge, the tip of it twitching back and forth. Flora didn't know what she would do without her cat. She was opinionated, loud, horribly spoiled, and only cuddled on her own terms, but her presence brought so much joy to Flora's life. Maybe being a crazy cat lady really was the way to go, but instead of getting five cats, she could focus all her attention on further spoiling just one.

Suddenly, the cat sat up and stared at the apartment door with interest, one ear flicking to the side as Flora sat up. The next moment, Amaretto jumped to the floor and trotted over to the door. That was all the warning Flora had before someone knocked.

She looked around her apartment with dread. It was a relatively nice place in one of the more upscale areas of Chicago, with high ceilings and a balcony that looked out over Lake Michigan.

It was also, currently, trashed. She'd had a real pity party this weekend, and there were leftover takeout containers lying around, along with tissues from all of the crying she had done, and a pile of the clothes Kyle had left behind that she was torn between throwing in the trash or lighting on fire. She would have opted for the latter, but she was pretty sure a balcony fire would get the fire department called on her.

The person at the door knocked again, more sharply this time. Flora rose to her feet slowly, mentally running through the list of who it could be. Her parents wouldn't visit without calling her first. They scheduled *everything.* Her brother wasn't even in the state. It might be her sister, but she'd been pretty annoyed when Flora backed out of the dinner at the last moment, and she hadn't told any of her family about her breakup so it couldn't be a pity visit. The same went for her friends—no one would just stop by without calling or texting first, even if she had told them about her imploded relationship.

Maybe it was her ex. Her eyes narrowed at the door as the knock sounded a third time. Whoever was on the other side sounded like they were getting annoyed. She was tempted just to ignore it, but the need to confirm who it was won out.

Moving slowly so whoever was in the hall wouldn't hear her footsteps, she approached the door and pressed one eye close to the peephole. The identity of her visitor had caught her off guard. She had *not* expected her Aunt Olivia to come visiting, of all people. The woman lived in California, for goodness' sakes!

Her surprise had her opening the door before the

state of her apartment could stop her. Her aunt, an intimidating woman who was a good five inches taller than Flora and always dressed to the nines, looked her up and down. She looked unimpressed with what she saw and brushed past Flora and into the apartment without a word, ignoring Amaretto as the cat twined around her feet. The look on her face only darkened when she took in the mess. Even if there hadn't been trash and clothes lying around, the drawn curtains gave the normally well-lit apartment a depressing feel.

"*What* has gotten into you, girl?"

"I—" The word came out as a croak, and Flora cleared her throat before trying again. "What are you doing here, Aunt Olivia? Is everything all right?"

Dread curdled in her stomach. The only reason she could imagine for her aunt's unexpected visit was if something disastrous had happened to her parents.

"Did it completely slip your mind that I was flying in for the weekend?" her aunt asked. "That *was* the point of the dinner you skipped, unless you've forgotten."

Flora gulped. She *had* forgotten. She'd put the dinner into her calendar app simply as *Family dinner.* They had them at least once a month, usually, and the fact that this one was special had slipped her mind in the face of Kyle's betrayal.

"Sorry. I've had a lot going on." Slowly, she closed the door behind her. Even though she was thirty, her aunt somehow still had the power to make her feel like a misbehaving child. All her life, her Aunt Olivia had been a sort of untouchable force of nature she was equal parts awed by and terrified of.

"So I see." She looked around the room again, and her face softened. "Come sit down with me, Flora. Tell me what's going on."

Flora joined her aunt on the couch, her guilt over missing the dinner enough to make her open up, even though talking about it hurt.

"Remember Kyle? I brought him to the family's Christmas celebration last year. I've been dating him for the last few years." Her aunt nodded, so Flora pressed on. "Well, I found out he's been cheating on me pretty much through our whole relationship. There were some other things too, and, well, it's just been really horrible. I'm sorry I didn't go to the dinner, but I didn't think I could make myself function like a normal person, and I didn't want to break down in tears during the third course."

"That's not all, though, is it?" her aunt asked. Flora stared at her, a little stung, because her aunt was acting like finding out someone you loved for *four years* had been betraying you for that entire time was nothing. Aunt Olivia shook her head, almost looking disappointed. "Flora, dear, you were the happiest girl I knew when you were younger. Maybe it's not as noticeable to the rest of your family, since they see you more often than I do, but every year I've seen a little more of that light dim from your eyes. You've gone from being a joy and a terror, to looking like you're just trudging through life. Maybe this breakup was a catalyst, but you can't tell me it's the only reason you're miserable. Tell me, Flora. Why are you sad?"

Flora blinked, feeling her throat swell with tears. She swallowed, and a moment later, she found herself pouring everything out to her aunt. How she felt like she'd made a mistake ever since the moment she chose her major, how the walls seemed to close in more and more every single day she went to work. "I feel so *trapped*," she admitted at last, in a whisper. "I don't know what to do. I hate my life, but I have no idea how to change anything."

Aunt Olivia nodded, somehow still looking unruffled despite Flora's breakdown. "I understand."

She blinked. "You do?"

Her aunt smiled, an expression that was a little

regretful and a little wistful. "I went through a similar crisis when I was a little younger than you. I was unhappy in the life I had built for myself but didn't have the means to change it. I was able to turn my life around thanks to my grandmother. She helped me then." She met Flora's eyes. "And I'm going to pass it forward to you, now."

"What do you mean?"

"I'm going to give you the means to change your life. Money, because that's what it always comes down to. Enough to build a new future for yourself." Flora stared at her, too stunned to think of anything to say. Her aunt patted her hand. "It's not free, of course. It's a loan, and you'll have two years to start paying it back. And it comes with some conditions. First, you need to make real changes in your life. Get out of this city. Quit your job. Move on from all of this. Second, you need to move forward with an eye on the future. You can't use this money to travel the world and goof off for two years. You need to use it to build something that will support you for the rest of your life. I *do* expect to be paid back. And third, you need to use it to follow your dreams. I'll be very disappointed if you're just as miserable in two years as you are now."

Flora gaped at her aunt. It was too much, what the older woman was offering. She should turn it down.

She'd been raised not to accept handouts, and even if this was technically a loan, it felt too close to one.

But she *was* miserable, and the deal her aunt had laid out filled her with something she hadn't felt for a long time. Hope. Joy. The chance at a brighter future and the ability to leave her mistakes in the past.

She accepted the deal.

CHAPTER TWO

Warbler, Kentucky. Flora clutched her steering wheel as she giddily took in her new town. It couldn't have been more different from Chicago, and that was a good thing. Flora enjoyed living in the city, but she knew her aunt was right. She wouldn't be able to make any real changes while she was surrounded by the same people and places she'd spent years stagnating around.

Warbler was tiny, but cute. She had already passed a number of old churches and beautiful historical buildings. There must be a gardening club in town, because neatly potted and planted flowers were everywhere. It was a weekend, and pedestrians were out in force. Flora could hardly wait to join them. There was the grocery store, where she would do her shopping, and there was a hardware store. She was sure she would need that, so she made a mental note of its location.

Then, her eyes landed on a coffee shop. It was a tiny building, standing detached from the others on a corner with a sign hanging above the door that read, *Violet Delights*, with an artistic rendering of a coffee cup with steam rising from the inside in the shape of flowers.

She was only minutes away from seeing her new house, but she had been driving since dawn and she was exhausted. She needed coffee. She needed caffeine. She needed it right now.

She pulled into a parking lot just around the corner from the coffee shop and made sure the truck was securely locked before she crossed the street and let herself into the building. The second she stepped inside, she was hooked. Everything was done in shades of purple, and it smelled amazing, like freshly roasted coffee beans and caramel.

A woman with long black hair was behind the counter, chatting with a man who looked like he was in his fifties or sixties. When she glanced over at Flora, she realized even the woman's *eyes* were purple. She was wearing contacts, of course, but Flora was impressed at the dedication to the coffee shop's theme. Her own hazel eyes felt boring by comparison.

"Hi, welcome to Violet Delights. I'm Violet, and you're new here. What can I get you?" Her voice was brusque, and she seemed to want to get the order out of the way as quickly as possible.

Flora scanned the menu quickly and said, "I'll take a medium white chocolate caramel latte."

She paid, then moved to the end of the counter to wait. Violet began heating up the milk for her latte, then sighed and pulled her phone out of her apron pocket when it chirped.

"It's him again," she said to the older man as she read the screen. "I guess he's walking home, since I can't give him a ride. It's going to take him forever, his friend lives miles out of town. I hope it rains on him."

The older man chuckled. "So do I. I'm sorry this backfired on you, Violet."

"It's not your fault, Uncle Gordon," Violet said. She shoved her phone back into her pocket and returned her attention to making the latte. "Just please, never hire anyone I'm dating ever again."

Flora tried to ignore the conversation she was obviously not intended to be a part of, but their exchange seemed to be over. Violet glanced up at her.

"So, you visiting someone or just passing through?"

"I'm moving here, actually. I just bought a house."

"Oh? Where?"

"A mile or two outside of town. I haven't actually seen it yet." Flora tried to smile without showing how nervous she was. "I'm just hoping my phone doesn't lose its service before I get there. I'm going to be completely lost if it does."

"What road is it on?" Violet asked. Flora told her, and the other woman replied, "You'll be fine, it's practically a straight shot out of town. Just follow Main Street until you hit your turn. You literally can't get lost."

Flora thanked her, but Violet's phone had chimed again, and the other woman barely looked at her as she handed the latte over and said, "Have a nice day."

Flora didn't care. She had her coffee. It was time to go to her house. Her new *home*, at least for the next two years.

Back in her truck, she sipped her latte and paused for a moment to appreciate how good it was, then pulled out of the parking lot and followed her phone's directions, which led her through town and out the other side. She passed by a small graveyard, then it was all hills and fields and trees. She rolled down her window to let the warm May air in, and when she slowed to follow a curve in the road, she could hear the drone of insects. The air was fresh and smelled alive, somehow. She inhaled deeply, banking the embers of happiness in her chest. The last two months had been a whirlwind, but despite everything—despite Kyle—she had been happier than she had been for longer than she wanted to admit to herself.

She hadn't been sure what she wanted to do, at first. The loan her aunt had given her was substantial enough to be intimidating. It was a good thing her aunt had given her the terms she had, because Flora's first thought was to get a one-way ticket to Europe and give herself the vacation of a lifetime while she tried to figure things out.

Instead of doing that, she had sat down in front of her laptop with Amaretto curled up beside her, and she had started to research. She must have looked up hundreds of jobs and business ideas, but nothing stuck, not until she turned the TV on during one of her breaks and flipped the channel to one of her favorite shows, which followed a couple who flipped houses.

She loved watching them work on old, neglected houses and turn them into something beautiful. They were honest about how hard the work was and how much capital it took to get started, but the work seemed so *satisfying*. They made their vision come to life, then sold the house and got to do it all over again. It might be hard work, but it was all they did. They didn't spend hour after hour in an office, trying to impress superiors who only cared about numbers or feeling guilty about every personal day they took. They were working for *themselves*, which Flora thought would make all the difference.

She had the idle thought of how fun house flipping would be, but then froze when she realized it didn't have to be an idle thought. She had the money to do it now. She had the freedom and time to turn this odd passion of hers into a reality.

More research was necessary, of course, but in the end, Flora had been hooked from the first second the thought occurred to her. Finding the right house to start her new career had taken longer, but here she was, finally. She'd bought the house not quite sight unseen — a helpful real estate agent had toured it and sent her a video and plenty of photos — but this would be the first time she'd seen it in person.

She followed the paved road until her phone's GPS chirped at her to turn left. Somehow sensing they were getting close, Amaretto let out a loud yowl from her carrier in the back seat.

"We'll be there soon," Flora promised. The cat wasn't a fan of car rides, but thankfully, her meows had subsided after the first hour of driving.

She turned onto a dirt road and passed by weathered wooden fences, open rolling fields, and, as she neared the house, trees that grew so close to the road they seemed to be practically climbing into it.

Then the trees stopped and, in an overgrown yard settled in the dip between two woodsy hills, she saw her house.

It wasn't pretty. The once white wooden siding was peeling and faded, and the porch roof sagged in the middle. The roof was missing shingles, and the gravel driveway was so overgrown as to be almost nonexistent. The property included several acres, but none of it had been tended for years, and even the grassy parts looked half-wild. A broken foundation of cinder blocks was all that remained of what had once been the garage. There was a small shed behind the house which looked like it would fall over if someone breathed on it wrong.

All of this she had seen in the pictures, but it was a little more intimidating in person. Doubt filled her for a single heartbeat, but she pushed past the feeling and pulled into the driveway with determination. Maybe too much determination. Her front driver's side wheel dipped into an unseen pothole with enough force to make her teeth clack together, and the trailer with all of her worldly goods in it rattled as it followed her new-to-her truck.

"We can put fixing the driveway on the list," she told Amaretto as she came to a stop next to the house. There was only one other house in view, a large house in much better condition than hers nestled in the trees on the other side of a field maybe an eighth of a mile further down and across the road from her. She knew from satellite images that there was another house down the road, just out of view around a curb, and of course, she had passed a few homesteads on her way out of town, which itself was only a few miles away. But to someone who had lived in one city or another all her life, she felt astonishingly alone.

It wasn't a bad feeling.

She shut off the engine and just sat there for a moment, listening to the drone of insects and chirps of birds and frogs. There was a pond somewhere on the property, according to the listing, which meant there would probably be a lot of insects as summer progressed.

It felt … peaceful.

"We're here," she told Amaretto. "Home sweet home, at least for the next two years." She had that long to get this place fixed up and sold. Then, she needed to start paying her aunt back and move on to her next house.

She had been assured the place was technically livable, though her real estate agent had had a weird note in his voice when he told her that. If she was doing this, she wanted to be all in, which meant living here while she fixed it up.

It was terrifying. It was exciting. She felt *alive.*

She got out of the truck and, with Amaretto's carrier in one hand, she walked toward the house. The porch steps gave her pause, and they creaked alarmingly when she climbed them, but they held. She crossed the porch, making another mental note about figuring out what to do for the dry, cracked wood, and came to a stop in front of the door. Putting Amaretto's carrier down, she took her phone out of her back pocket and double-checked her real estate agent's last email, in which he had given her the code for the key safe on the doorknob. She punched it in and held her breath, grateful when the little box popped open.

She took the key out with careful fingers and used it to turn the dead bolt, which slid back with a *clunk.*

After putting both the key and her phone back into

her pockets, she stooped to pick up Amaretto's carrier before she turned the doorknob and pushed the door open.

Taking a deep breath, she stepped into her house for the first time.

And immediately frowned, looking first at the puddle of water on the floor, and then at the matching stain on the ceiling above her head.

"Is the roof leaking?"

CHAPTER THREE

Flora edged past the puddle on the hardwood floor and moved further into the house. It smelled dusty and old, and the peeling wallpaper gave it a haunted house feel that she wasn't sure she liked, but despite all of that, there was a heavy sense of peace about the place. It was quiet, no traffic or other people's music or shouting, just the twittering of birds from outside … and the steady *plunk* of the water that was still dripping from the ceiling.

Ignoring that for now, she put Amaretto's carrier down in the hallway, safely out of reach of the dripping water. "Sit tight for just a few more minutes, sweetie. I'm going to grab your litter box, and then I'll get a room set up for you."

She retrieved the cat's supplies from the rental

trailer and explored the first floor until she found the small room that had been labelled as either an office or potential fourth bedroom on the listing. It opened off of the living room. There was a built-in bookshelf on one wall, and a single window on the adjacent wall that looked out to the trees that bordered the side edge of the property. The room was bare and dusty, but after checking the corners and edges of the room, Flora was satisfied it would do for now. At least there was nothing Amaretto could get into. After learning she had a cat, her real estate agent had been kind enough to warn her that the house's previous owner had left rat poison behind. She would have to make sure it was *thoroughly* cleaned out before the cat got free range of the place.

She set up the litterbox with fresh litter in one corner and placed Amaretto's plush bed in the opposite side of the room before going to the kitchen to fill the cat's special water fountain with water from the tap. The tap gurgled and sputtered for a few worrying seconds before running clear. The water had been tested and deemed safe prior to the sale, so she filled the dish with only a moment's hesitation, then returned to the office and plugged it in to the wall. The water started flowing with a quiet bubbling sound that made her feel just a little more at home.

A few minutes later, she was sitting cross-legged in front of the closed door while Amaretto walked slowly around the room, pausing to sniff at the walls or floor every few steps. Flora had spooned a little canned food into the cat's food dish, but she was ignoring the snack in favor of exploring.

"It's just temporary," Flora said, feeling bad. "You'll be able to roam around the whole house soon, I promise. I know it's scary, but it'll feel like home in no time. Plus, I'll be around a lot more. No more going into the office every day and leaving you alone. Won't that be nice?"

She knew she was mostly just talking to calm herself down. She was excited about her new lease on life, but being here made it all too real and a little terrifying. A little lonely, too. She had a feeling she was going to be spending a lot of time by herself and was more grateful than ever for the cat's company.

A rumble of thunder made her stand up and walk over to the window to look at the sky. It had been clear when she got here, but now she could see grey clouds looming low in the distance.

"Hope this place doesn't come down on my head if it storms," she muttered. Of course, the house had been standing this long—nearly a hundred years, according to its listing—so it would probably keep standing a while longer. Still, it was going to be a big change from the modern apartment she was used to.

With a last assurance to Amaretto that she would be back soon, Flora left the room, shutting the door quietly behind her, then started exploring the house. The first floor consisted of the small office room, a half bath, a living room, and the kitchen, which had a door that opened to the backyard. There was a door to the basement, but when she tried the light switch at the top of the stairs, nothing happened, so she decided to tackle *that* part of the exploration later. Instead, she went up the narrow staircase to the second floor.

There were three bedrooms up here, along with the only full bathroom in the house. She wondered if she could hire someone to put a shower in the downstairs bathroom. If a family bought this house when it came time to sell it, they would probably want more than one full bathroom in the place.

She determined the master bedroom by the size of it. The other two bedrooms were smaller, but not as cramped as the tiny one downstairs that she had already determined would be an office. It was in one of the two small bedrooms that she found the leak in the ceiling. Even she, with her limited knowledge of how houses worked, could tell it had been going on for a while. The floorboards were warped and soft under the soggy mess of the ceiling. Parts of the plaster were falling down, and it was still dripping from whenever it had rained last.

Somehow, *this* particular issue had been glossed over by her real estate agent. Or … maybe she had just missed it in the face of everything else. The person who inspected the house had sent her a *very* thick packet with everything he had found, and she was sure she had missed some things. This was just … a very big thing to have missed.

"Right, there's a leaky roof. And it's about to rain." She eyed the dripping ceiling and the puddle on the floor, the puddle that had a twin on the first level. It was going to get worse, that was certain. She knew she didn't have a hope of fixing the hole in the roof before the storm hit, but … maybe a tarp? She could do this. It was her first big stumbling block, but if she managed to patch the leak at least temporarily, that was good, right? At least the water damage wouldn't get any worse while she tried to figure out a more permanent fix.

Of course, she didn't currently *have* a tarp, but she knew where the hardware store was, and she even had a truck, so she could buy a big ladder and bring it back with her too. She'd need a ladder anyway, for all the repairs she had to do, so it wasn't like it would be a waste of money.

The air was heavy and humid with the coming storm by the time she had unhitched the trailer from her truck. She didn't have time to unload it before going into town, so she would have to wait until tomorrow to return it to the nearest rental company. It would cost her another twenty dollars, but there was nothing she could do about it.

As she pulled away from the house, she looked at it in the rearview mirror. Sure enough, she could see a spot on the roof where some of the shingles had fallen away. The house looked a little more beaten down than it had when she first pulled up and gazed at it with rose-tinted glasses, and she felt another tremor of doubt, but she bolstered herself against it.

She could do this. She *had* to do this. She was going to build herself a new life, and a happy future.

And the first step was finding a tarp before the storm hit.

CHAPTER FOUR

She managed to find her way back to the hardware store without using her GPS, which felt like a small victory. The roads were a lot less busy than she was used to, which made it easier for her to pay attention to landmarks, like the graveyard. In fact, the only other vehicle she saw on her way into town was a white cargo van that blasted past her like it had somewhere to be in a hurry. It was strange, after the chaos of Chicago's streets. Strange, but nice.

Warbler seemed to have a simple layout, with most of the businesses focused around the main intersection in town. She didn't have time to explore it today, but was looking forward to touring the town tomorrow, after she had returned the trailer.

She pulled up along the curb in front of the hardware store, glad that there was ample parking since she still wasn't used to the size of the vehicle she had replaced her sensible sedan with. It felt weird to own a pickup truck, but she already knew she wanted to learn how to do most of the work on her house herself, which meant she needed a way to transport tools and supplies.

Upon entering Brant's Hardware and Garden Supplies, Flora felt like she was transported back in time. The store looked like it was at least as old as her house, with its creaky floor and crowded aisles. She felt lost the instant she was through the door. *Tarps*, she thought. *Where would they keep tarps?* She would probably need nails too, to keep it down. Or maybe a staple gun? She had seen tarps on people's roofs before, and it seemed like a simple enough idea in concept, but now that she was actually here, it suddenly seemed like a huge task. Maybe she should just buy a big plastic bucket to catch the drips for now and let a professional worry about putting a stop to the leak.

She was eyeing some orange plastic buckets that were stacked in a pile near the store's entrance when a gruff voice said, "What're you looking for?"

She looked up to see an elderly man squinting at

her from behind the register. He had been so quiet, she hadn't even realized he was there.

"Um, I think I'm looking for tarps? My roof is leaking, and—"

"Speak up," he snapped. "I can't hear you when you're mumbling like that."

"Tarps!" she said, raising her voice. "Do you sell tarps?"

"Grady!" he shouted, making her jump. "Got someone looking for tarps!"

Footsteps creaked across the floor, and a moment later, a man about Flora's age came around the end of an aisle. He had light brown hair that was just long enough to fall into his eyes, eyes that met Flora's for long enough that she could tell they were a startling shade of blue before he looked away again. *He's cute*, she thought, then shoved that thought down *hard.* She wasn't even close to ready to think about dating again. Right now, all she could afford to think about was finding a way to keep her house from flooding. More thunder rumbled in the distance, deep enough she could have sworn she felt it in her very bones.

"Tarps are in the back," he grunted, turning to lead her down the aisle.

She followed, feeling a little out of her depth as she looked at all of the tools and supplies around her.

It wasn't as if she had never been in a hardware store before, but it had only been for simple projects, like picking up some paint or buying some nails to hang a picture on the wall. She had watched a lot of videos about do-it-yourself home repairs before she bought the house, but she knew there was a big difference between watching someone else do something and doing it herself.

"What size are you looking for?"

"Huh?" She quickly reoriented herself on her current task. "Oh, just a small one, I think?" The damaged part of the roof wasn't that big.

"You going to be storing it outside? You'll want a UV resistant one if you are."

They rounded the corner and came to a stop in front of a shelving unit that contained nothing but tarps. Flora stared at it, beginning to feel overwhelmed again.

"Yeah, it's for my roof. So, I guess one that's resistant to sunlight would be good? I don't know how long it will take to get someone out to repair the roof properly."

He was reaching for the plastic package but paused and glanced at her again. "You sure you want a small one?"

"There's only a few shingles missing," Flora said,

wishing she had thought to take a picture of the damaged area. "I'm sure even your smallest tarp would be overkill."

He shifted, crossing his arms and looking at her skeptically. "You ever patched a roof before?"

She shook her head. "It seems pretty self-explanatory, though. I'll need a ladder too, by the way. I figure I just have to nail the tarp over the hole and then I'm good to go, right? At least until I get someone out to fix it properly."

The look in his eyes had her doubting herself. "Where is the hole? At the peak of your roof?"

"No, it's further down, closer to the eaves than the peak, I'd say."

"Then just slapping a tarp over the hole won't do you much good. You need to tarp everything above it too, or the water will get underneath."

It seemed obvious, now that he said it. Water flowed down, after all – just nailing a tarp over the hole wouldn't do much other than keep rain from falling directly in. All the rain that landed on the roof above it would just go under the tarp. She flushed. "Okay, then I guess I need a big tarp." If it needed to go all the way up over the peak of the roof... "Whatever your biggest size is."

He gave her a skeptical look but grabbed a

different tarp from the shelf. She was surprised by how heavy it was when he handed it to her. "Thanks. I'll need some nails too."

He shook his head. "You're going to want screws. Good deck screws." He turned, leading the way to another aisle, where he found a big box of screws and handed that to her as well. She was beginning to wish she had grabbed a cart. He paused, frowning. "Do you have a drill? Lumber?"

"No, I haven't bought a drill yet. I wanted to do some more research, figure out what brand is good…" She trailed off, looking from his face down to the screws. "But I guess I'm going to need one for this, aren't I?" She did own a screwdriver set, but she wasn't sure if it would even be possible to screw all of these into the roof by hand. "And what do I need lumber for?"

He was beginning to look a little annoyed. "Strapping. Keeps the screws from ripping out of the tarp."

She looked down at the supplies in her arms again. She thought of the bucket, which would have been a much, much easier solution to her problem. This was turning out to be a bigger project than she had expected, but she didn't want to call it quits yet. Maybe she could get a bucket for today, and then get to work on the roof once the storm blew over.

"All right," she said with a sigh. "I guess I'm getting a drill today. And wood. And a ladder. Can't forget the ladder."

She detoured to grab a cart first, then met Grady in the aisle where he had told her the drills were. He put two boxes in her cart without a word, and she said, "Wait. I want to make sure I get a good drill. I'm going to be doing a lot of work myself. What brand is this? I need to look up the reviews. And why are there two boxes?"

He sighed. "The battery comes separate. It's a good brand. Not the most expensive, but reliable. It'll last."

She hesitated but decided to take him at his word. He had already proven he knew a lot more about all of this than she did. He helped her select a ladder next, a lightweight aluminum one that could extend up to thirty feet. Even collapsed, it would have to stick out of the back of her truck, so she ended up with a set of ratchet straps as well, along with an orange flag to tie to the back of it. The lumber, thankfully, she didn't have to cart around with her. He told her his boss would ring it up at the register, and he would load it into her truck for her. Of course, that discussion led to her getting a handsaw as well, since she might need to *cut* the pieces of wood.

Finally, she stomped back toward the register, paused to throw one of the big, orange buckets into her cart—she kind of wished she had just done that from the beginning, but she was too stubborn to back out of this project now—and started checking out. The elderly man rang up her things. Through the window, she could see Grady putting the lengths of lumber into her truck. *It's okay,* she told herself. *I knew this was going to be hard work. I can do this.*

She paid with her new debit card. It was linked directly to the account that held the money her aunt had loaned her. She had her own savings that she was keeping separate from that for her personal expenses, but she wanted to be able to keep track of exactly how she spent her aunt's money. She hoped she wouldn't go through the entire loan, since she knew she would be paying every cent she spent back.

She accepted her receipt from the man, then pushed her cart outside. Grady somehow already had the ladder and the wood all strapped down in the back of her truck with the orange safety flag attached to the load. She put her other items in the back of the cab, then turned to push the cart back into the store only to find Grady in her way. That skeptical look was back on his face. "You got someone to help you?"

"With the roof? No. But I can figure it out. I'll

watch some videos, learn how to do it properly. If I can't get it done before the storm hits, I'll just have to stick the bucket under the hole and call it good for today. But I'll know what I'm doing by the time tomorrow rolls around." She laughed, but he just frowned.

"You shouldn't do roofing work on your own."

"Why?" she asked, crossing her own arms. "I know I don't seem prepared, but I can figure it out. I can learn. Women can be good at fixing things too, you know."

"It's not that," he said with a snort. "It's just a dumb idea. You've got to at least have someone around who can call an ambulance if you fall off and break your leg."

"Oh." She deflated slightly. Once again, she knew he was right. She really hadn't thought this through.

"Just … invite a friend over to help you, all right?" He rubbed the back of his neck, looking embarrassed. "I'd feel bad if I heard you got yourself killed trying to do this on your own."

"Right," she said, faltering. "It's just … I just moved here. Today, that is. I don't know anyone. Do you think there's someone I could hire … or … could I hire *you* to come and help me? You seem to know what you're doing."

He glanced back at the hardware store and seemed to come to a decision. "I'll be right back."

With that, he took her cart and pushed it back into the store, leaving her standing outside. She leaned against her truck, sighing. She had bought all of this, and for what? A project she couldn't even complete on her own. She really needed to be more realistic about what she couldn't do by herself.

Grady returned only a minute later, though his name tag was missing and he had keys on a lanyard in his hand. "I'll follow you back," he offered. "Help you unload the truck and take a look at the roof. I don't think we can get much done before the storm hits, but I can come back tomorrow to help you, if you want."

She brightened. "Really? Is it okay for you to leave your shift early?"

He shrugged. "The old man doesn't care. We won't get much business anyway, once it starts storming. Ready to go?"

"Yeah. I'm not far out of town—just follow me." She smiled at him. "Thanks. I mean it. And thanks for warning me. I didn't even think about what would happen if I fell off the roof and got hurt."

He just grunted and squinted at the sky. "Better get going. It's going to be a bad storm."

That seemed like a good reason to hurry to her. She climbed into her truck and started the engine, still unused to how powerful it sounded compared to her old car. She grinned a little, thinking of the look on her mother's face when Flora rolled up to their house in her new vehicle. Her parents had both been doubtful about her new path in life, but somehow, her aunt had taken care of the worst of their objections. They had been upset when they learned she had quit her accounting job, but she knew they just wanted her to be happy and successful. She hoped to show them that successful didn't have to mean sitting in an office for eight hours every day until she was grey and wrinkled.

Another, older pickup truck with a dented grille pulled around from the back of the building, and she saw Grady in the driver's seat. He came to a stop in the road—something that wouldn't have been possible without a lot of honking in Chicago—and waited for her to pull out ahead of him.

She drove back through town and had barely reached the edge of it before drops of rain started pattering down onto her windshield. It was only a couple raindrops every second, but from how dark the sky had gotten, she knew it was just a matter of time until a downpour started. She pressed on the gas a little, wanting to at least reach her house before it started pouring in earnest.

They were out of town and heading toward the turn onto the dirt road that led to her new house—and despite how much she had misjudged this particular project, the thought still sent a wave of giddiness through her—when she saw something along the side of the road. Something that stood out against the greenery. Something blue and bright red.

She stomped on her brakes and jerked the wheel over so she came to a stop half off the road. Grady's truck swung past hers and came to a stop along the side of the road in front of her. She scrabbled at her seatbelt, undoing it and opening her door in almost the same motion. Ignoring the rain that was beginning to come down harder, she ran back down the road to where she had seen the too-bright colors just off the road.

She hadn't been imagining things. There was a man lying in the ditch, his face upturned to the sky, his eyes open and unblinking even as the rain began to fall harder.

CHAPTER FIVE

Flora knelt down next to the man, not sure what to do. He was all scraped up, as if he had gone rolling across the road. She could only guess he had been hit by a car, and wondered how someone could hit a person with their car and not even stop.

She heard Grady approach from behind her. "What did you do that for? I almost hit you—" He broke off. "Oh." There was silence for a moment until he said, "I don't have a cell phone. You should—"

"The police, right. Yeah," she muttered. She stood up, and turning her back to the dead man, returned to her truck. She had left her phone in the cup holder, and pulled it out now, feeling sick and cold as she unlocked the screen and navigated to the phone app. She pressed the numbers for 911 for the first time in her life and then walked back to stare down at the man as the call rang through to the dispatcher.

She felt far away from herself as she stumbled over her words to tell the brusque woman on the line what she had found. A man, lying on the side of the road. Seemingly the victim of a hit and run. Dead.

She had to ask Grady for the name of the road they were on, since she couldn't remember, and then she had to follow the dispatcher's instructions to check to see if the man was breathing, fighting back the urge to cry when she found nothing. The police and ambulance were on their way, but she knew in her gut it was already too late. The man was dead. There was nothing she could do.

With a crack of thunder, the rain began to pour down in earnest.

She heard the sirens long before she saw the flashing lights through the downpour. The ambulance got there first, blocking the lane when it parked. She and Grady were both soaked to the bone, but even though he had suggested she wait in her nice, *dry* truck while he stood guard next to the man, she had refused. What was a little rain? It didn't seem to matter at all in the face of a man's death. She stood back while the paramedics crouched near the man, checking for his vital signs with more confidence than she had. While they searched for signs of life, a police cruiser pulled up in front of Grady's truck, and an officer got out. He didn't walk back to them right away; instead, he lingered around the front of Grady's truck for a few moments before he headed their way.

He crouched near the body, examining the dead man and talking to the paramedics in a hushed tone. It felt like a long time but was only a few minutes before he stood back up and approached Flora and Grady.

"Either of you injured?" he asked, glancing only fleetingly at Flora before turning to Grady. "Hands behind your back. You're going to be coming back to the station."

Grady glowered at the man but did as he was told as the officer clapped handcuffs onto him.

"What are you doing?" Flora asked. She tried to ignore the way the paramedics were loading the other man's body onto a stretcher and covering him with a sheet. "He didn't do anything."

"I don't know where you're from, but around here we take vehicular manslaughter seriously," the officer said.

"Grady didn't hit the man," Flora said. "Neither of us did." She added the last as an afterthought, suddenly worried he would take her in too.

"Ma'am, his truck is damaged in a way that is consistent with a collision. He is here, at the scene of the crime, and has a documented history of conflict with the deceased. I appreciate you stopping and calling for help, but we can take it from here."

"No," she said, frustrated. "You don't understand. He was working at the hardware store and only just now got off his shift to come help me. He was following me to my house when I saw the man on the side of the road. It's literally impossible that he's the one who hit him."

The officer hesitated, glancing from the body to Grady, then over at Grady's truck. At last, he shook his head. "Miss, you'll have to come to the station to give your statement. We'll figure this out, but this isn't the time or place for it. Not with this weather."

"But –"

"It's okay," Grady muttered. "Just leave it."

Flora watched, gaping, as the officer led Grady to his patrol vehicle and put him in the back. She had never seen anyone get arrested before. The paramedics were already loading the dead man into the ambulance, and then they'd go to the hospital or the morgue or wherever bodies went in a town this tiny. Everything seemed rushed, and she wasn't sure if that was because she was in shock, or because everyone was nervous about the storm.

She stood there until the officer returned, hunched against the wind and rain. "I'm Officer Hendricks. This isn't any sort of place to take a real statement, not with the rain coming down like this. I'll take your name and contact information here, then, you're going to need to follow me back to the station so we can figure out what happened here." She gave him her name and her phone number, along with her new address when she remembered she hadn't changed her driver's license yet. It seemed like an eternity before she climbed back into her truck. Dripping wet, she sat there, staring blankly out the window until the officer started his patrol car and did a U-turn on the road, heading back toward town. She followed him.

She had never given a statement to the police before, but she was determined to keep her wits about her and do her best. It wasn't fair for Grady to be handcuffed like that. He hadn't done anything wrong, and she was going to prove it.

CHAPTER SIX

The Warbler police station was small, lit with flickering overhead lights, and held a lingering smell of old coffee. Officer Hendricks took Grady to the back while the woman at the front desk managed to scrounge up some towels for Flora, so she could at least begin to get dry.

Before long, Officer Hendricks returned to lead her to his office, where he gestured for her to take a seat in a chair that looked to be as old as she was.

"So, you're new to town," he said conversationally. "I'd heard someone bought that old house. Welcome to Warbler, though I'm sure this isn't the kind of welcome you were hoping for."

"Not really," she admitted. She shivered, wrapping her arms around herself—the police station was air-conditioned, and after being soaked from the rain, it was chilly.

"Well, I know it might not seem that way at the moment, but this is a good town with good people. Mostly. If you're looking for help with the house, I can recommend better people than Grady Barnes. If you need a contractor, Gordon Hatfield is always a good way to go." He sighed. "He'll be crushed when he hears about Troy, even after their falling out."

"Sorry, Troy?"

"Right, you're not from around here. The man you found was Troy Bartlett." He shook his head. "Poor guy. He had his issues around town, but he was one of us. He grew up here. Now his life is over before it was meant to be, and Grady's going to be behind bars for who knows how long. Two lives, wrecked, just like that. And here I thought Grady was going to do better than his good-for-nothing brother."

"I told you, he didn't do it," Flora said. "Look, Grady was at the hardware store when I got there, and I'm sure his boss could tell you how long he was working before I showed up. He helped me figure out what I needed to buy, and then he offered to help me unload the lumber I bought and take a look at my roof so I didn't kill myself trying to do it on my own. He was following me the whole way from town. There's absolutely no way he could have hit that man, and I just met him—I have no reason to lie."

Officer Hendricks frowned. "I'm not saying I don't believe you, but I've been in this job a long time. If something seems obvious, it usually is, and a man with a dented truck and a grudge against the victim found at the scene of a fatal car accident is about as obvious as it gets. You do understand, if this goes to court, you might be asked to testify?"

"Yes," she said firmly. "Whatever happened, it didn't have anything to do with him." She paused. "Or me. I just bought that truck, I know there's no damage on the front bumper, and I certainly know I didn't hit anyone with it."

"Don't worry, you're not a suspect." He sighed and pinched the bridge of his nose. "We still need to question him, you understand that, right? If he and his boss verify your story and forensics doesn't find anything on his truck, we'll let him go. But if it does turn out you're lying to help him for some reason, you and I will be having another, less friendly chat."

"I'm not lying," she insisted. "So I'm not worried about it."

He sighed again, then said, "Well, why don't you walk me through everything that happened today, from the moment you left your house to go to the hardware store, ending with when you called the dispatcher. I'm going to be recording this, and it's possible we may use your statement in court. Before we begin, I'd like to remind you that lying or otherwise impeding a police investigation is a crime. Are you ready to start?"

She was. She told him everything, every detail she could remember, of her day. Her worries about the leaking roof seemed so small now.

Eventually, he told her she was free to go. Everything in the back of her truck was completely soaked, of course, and she could only hope the rain wouldn't hurt the lumber. She drove home, slowing as she passed the spot where she had spotted Troy's body. There were no skid marks on the road, which made her wonder if the person who hit him had even *seen* him.

She shook her head. Other than giving her statement to the police and being available if they needed her to testify, this didn't have anything to do with her. She was just an unfortunate witness. There was no use in wondering if she might have been able to save Troy's life if only she had left the hardware store a little earlier, or left her house a little later. She couldn't go back in time, and she couldn't change what had already happened.

Since everything was already soaking wet, and she didn't feel like risking the shed collapsing on her while she dragged the ladder and lumber into it, she left everything in her truck except for the bucket and hurried through the rain into her house. She peeled off her shoes and then went upstairs to put the bucket under the hole in the roof, which was already dripping water in a steady stream. She oriented the bucket so it would catch most of the splashes, then stared up at the ceiling with a sigh. Not only did she still feel it was unfair that Grady had been arrested, but she was also pretty sure it meant he wouldn't be coming out to help her with the roof tomorrow. Maybe she could post online and see if someone else was willing to help? That would mean accepting the help of a complete stranger, though. Sure, Grady was also a stranger, but she had at least spoken to him and knew where he worked and had been able to get enough of a feeling for him to know that he wasn't a complete weirdo. She wasn't quite desperate enough to start asking strangers online for help, not yet.

Maybe she could call that guy Officer Hendricks had mentioned, Gordon … something. He was a contractor, and she wasn't sure if that meant he did roof work or not, but maybe he would be able to point her in the right direction if he didn't.

She put a pin in the thought when she heard sad meows coming from downstairs. She returned to the bottom floor and let herself into Amaretto's room. The cat rushed up to greet her, but then gave Flora's wet clothing a disdainful sniff and backed away when Flora went to pet her.

"It's just a little rain, you brat," she muttered. She was too used to the cat's picky behavior for it to sting. Plus, she *was* soaking wet. She needed to change.

Of course, all of her clothes were still in the trailer. She left Amaretto in the office room and walked over to the window by the front door to peer outside. The rain was really coming down, and not just straight down, but blowing and gusting against the side of the house. She sighed.

"Well, I'm already wet. I might as well go for it."

She dashed outside to the trailer, yanked her suitcase out of it, and slammed the trailer door shut and, shrieking, ran back to the house. She couldn't do anything about the water on the floor – there was no way she was going back out there just to get her towels—but she did drag the suitcase into Amaretto's room. She left her wet clothes in a pile on the floor to be dealt with later and only relaxed when she was finally dressed in something dry and comfortable.

It was late now, late enough it would have been

getting dark even without the storm, and she was hungry and tired. She had some leftover snacks and drinks from her road trip, but they were still in the truck, and she didn't want to go back outside again, not after finally getting dry. She busied herself with spreading her clothing out on the kitchen counter. There was supposed to be a washer and dryer in the house, but she had a sinking feeling they were in the basement. The basement that didn't have any working lights. She considered going down there with her phone's flashlight, but decided she'd had enough adventure for one day. She was half afraid she'd get down the stairs only to discover that the basement was flooding, and she just couldn't deal with anything else today.

She decided to wait out the storm. Sitting in Amaretto's room with her back to the wall and the cat deigning to sit on her lap, she pulled up some videos about how to tarp over a hole on her roof on her phone and settled in to watch them.

She might not be able to do anything about it right now, but she could certainly learn. Tomorrow would be a new day, and she would be better prepared when it dawned.

CHAPTER SEVEN

Eventually, the storm eased until it was just drizzling outside. Flora hopefully flicked the porch light switch, but the light didn't come on, and when she poked her head outside, she saw that the light fixture was empty. Lightbulbs would have to go on her list, but first, she needed her notebook so she could *make* a list. On the upside, it wasn't raining hard enough to completely drench her anymore, so she hurried out to the truck to grab her snacks and drinks and brought in the bag of supplies from the hardware store for good measure. Then she ran to the trailer, rescuing her broom, a bag she thought was full of her bedding and another one she was pretty sure held towels, and a box of cleaning supplies. Back inside, she used some of the towels to mop up the water on the floor left over from the leaky roof and her own drenched clothes, then went upstairs and did the same for the splashes around the bucket, which was mostly doing its job and preventing further water damage to the floor.

She heaved the bucket into the bathroom, emptied it into the bathtub, then returned it to catch the remaining drips from the ceiling. Then, she went down to Amaretto's room and started sweeping. This tiny office room on the first floor was going to be her base of operations for now. She hadn't brought any furniture—her apartment had been fully furnished when she rented it, and it hadn't made sense to buy furniture in Chicago and then drive it all down to Kentucky with her. She'd have to get some necessities in the next day or two, but for now, she made a usable bed on the floor with her bedding and her pillow from home. She plugged her phone into the wall outlet, changed into her pajamas, and slipped under her comforter. The house was silent around her other than for the pattering of rain, and her heart was heavy with thoughts of the man she had been too late to help, but despite everything, she still had a glimmer of hope inside her. She settled down to sleep with Amaretto purring on her chest.

The next morning, she woke up with a stiff neck and sunshine streaming in through the window. Amaretto was perched on the windowsill, and the cat gave a cute trill as she twitched forward, following the shadow of a bird as it flew by. Flora smiled, glad that her cat, at least, was enjoying their new accommodations. She enjoyed the peaceful feeling of the morning for a few moments, then she got up and tried to remember which bag she had packed her toothbrush in.

An hour later, Flora was feeling mostly like herself. It felt strange to get ready in a house that was so empty it almost seemed to echo, but she kind of liked it. It made the house feel full of potential.

She ate some beef jerky for breakfast, then checked the fridge. The interior was disappointingly warm, but then she realized it was unplugged. With some huffing and puffing, she got it pulled away from the wall enough to plug it in and was relieved when it hummed to life. When she checked back again a few minutes later, it was already getting cold, so at least she could add some real groceries to her list.

Her list, which she still hadn't begun to make.

Since she didn't have any furniture, she just sat on the floor in Amaretto's room, her notebook balanced on her knees as she started writing out a shopping list.

Lightbulbs, a shower curtain, and food. She'd brought her pots and pans with her, at least, but she still needed to find and unpack them. At the bottom of the list, she scribbled—*Ask about contractor!*

She still needed to get her roof fixed, even if it was just a temporary fix. She also wanted to stop at the hardware store and make sure Grady had either been released, or if he hadn't, see if she could get some information about what was going on. She felt vaguely like his arrest had been her fault, since he wouldn't have been there if it wasn't for her. She hoped her statement had helped him, at the very least.

After giving Amaretto her breakfast, she grabbed her purse and put her shoes on, ready to go shopping, but then she spotted the trailer and remembered that she really should take it back today. Which meant she had to finish unpacking it before she could go anywhere.

She sighed and got to work carrying her boxes and bags in and leaving everything in a jumbled pile by the front door. She could take care of it later. Right now, she just wanted to get to town, get some supplies, and get some real food. Gas station snacks weren't going to cut it for much longer.

She dragged the wood and the ladder out of the back of her truck and laid it all along the side of her house, then hooked the now-empty trailer up to her truck – something she felt absurdly proud she now knew how to do. Backing the truck up with the trailer attached might be a little more difficult, but she would manage, she was pretty sure.

Before she could get into her truck, she heard the sound of tires on gravel and turned to look down the road. She hadn't seen any vehicles drive past her house yet, and with how quiet the road was, she was beginning to suspect the only people who used it were those who lived on it. She raised her hand to wave at her potential neighbor but faltered when she saw a familiar truck with a dented grill slowing to turn into her driveway.

"Grady?" she said when he got out of his truck. "What are you doing here? I didn't expect to see you today. Wait, how did you know where I live?"

He looked tired, but at least he wasn't in handcuffs or a jail cell.

"It wasn't hard to figure out," he said. "Only so many houses for sale out this way, and Officer Hendricks was chatty once he realized I hadn't done anything. I didn't have your number, and I wanted to make sure you weren't trying to fix up that roof on your own."

"I'm glad you came," she said. "I didn't think

you'd want to help me anymore, not after yesterday. I was just about to go into town, but if you think we can do the roof first, I'll go later. Officer Hendricks mentioned some guy—I think his name was Gordon—who might be able to help with the house, so I was going to ask him for help. But if you still want to help, that's even better!"

"Gordon Hatfield?" He scowled. "Stay away from him. He overcharges and does shoddy work."

She blinked. "Well, that's good to know." It probably shouldn't have been surprising that Grady knew who he was. This was a small town, after all. Things would be different here.

"Do you still want to do this yourself?" He eyed the roof. "We could probably get it done today."

"Yes, definitely," she said. "Let me get the ladder."

Ten minutes later, they were both standing on her roof. Now that she was up here, Flora was glad she had another person with her. She wasn't afraid of heights, but standing on a steep roof was a lot different from peering down out of her apartment's windows. Her legs felt a little shaky, but she ignored the vertigo and watched Grady examine the hole in the roof.

"I don't think the decking is rotted. Something damaged it, maybe a branch in a storm. It should be safe to walk up here, but watch your step. These shingles are old, and some are falling off."

Grady definitely knew what he was doing. He took the lead, but not in a way that felt bossy to Flora. He explained what he was doing as they spread out the tarp and wrapped the end around a length of the lumber twice before holding it still so she could screw it down. It was hard work—harder than she expected—but it was satisfying to be doing it with her own two hands. Next time it stormed, at least she wouldn't have to worry about her house flooding.

"I hope they let you go without too much trouble," she said while they were taking a short break, sitting on the top ridge of her roof and gazing out over the countryside.

"I guess it looked pretty bad," he admitted. "My family's lived here for decades." He shrugged. "They have a reputation, and my brother's in prison for a DUI. I think Hendricks was the one who arrested him. And he knows I knew Troy."

"He mentioned that to me. I take it you two weren't friends."

"Hardly," he snorted. "He was a competitor. I do

odd jobs like this on the side, and a while back, right after he split from Hatfield Contracting, he asked me for advice on what to charge his customers. Then he used what I told him to undercut all of my prices and took a lot of my work."

"Oh," she said. It was starting to make more sense why Officer Hendricks had thought Grady was involved in Troy's death. "I guess in a small town like this, everyone really does know everyone."

"Yep. There's no such thing as privacy in Warbler."

"So, who do you think hit him?" she asked. "I mean, do you think it was a local, or just someone driving through who wasn't paying attention?"

Grady shrugged. "It could have been anyone. I just know it wasn't me. I don't want to stick my nose in it any more than that."

Flora nodded. She was curious, but it also wasn't really any of her business. The police would handle the investigation. She had a roof to fix. She stood up and grabbed another piece of wood from where they had laid it out on the roof. The strapping went around the edges of the tarp, and the screws went through it to pin the tarp to the roof. By the time they were done, the whole thing would be about as wind and rain proof as it could get.

It wasn't a permanent fix, but it was going to be a very good temporary one. They were only halfway done installing the strapping, but already she felt a surge of pride as she looked over their work. This was just the beginning, and she had already learned so much.

CHAPTER EIGHT

It was early evening by the time they finished. The blue tarp spread out over her roof was an eyesore, but a waterproof eyesore she was very glad to have. Grady looked over the shed for her and announced it was "safe enough," so they stored the ladder and the scraps of wood inside, then Flora stepped back and admired their handiwork one last time. It looked like it would last through any storm that hit it. She just wished the house's previous owner had done something similar before the leak caused so much damage.

She thanked Grady and invited him in, but he said he had to get going. When she offered to pay him, he turned her down.

"Just keep me in mind if you need any more work done," he said.

"I will," she promised. She waved goodbye as he pulled out of the driveway, then, shooting one last appreciative look at the roof, she went back inside to grab her purse. She had her own errands to run and really wanted to get that trailer returned before the rental company closed. This time, when she looked at her house in the rearview mirror as she drove away, she didn't feel that yawning sensation that she might be in over her head. She'd faced her first big challenge and had overcome it, and the victory left her feeling like she could do anything.

She returned the trailer to the rental company one town over, then headed back into Warbler to run her errands. She was tired after the long day of physical labor, but she *needed* some real food.

When she spotted Violet Delights on her way to the grocery store, she only thought about it for a second before pulling over. She still had a lot she wanted to do tonight, and she could use an energy boost. The latte she'd had the day before had been good enough that she was looking forward to drinking another one.

When she walked in, Violet was behind the counter. Her black hair was pulled up into a ponytail today, but she was wearing the same purple contacts she had in yesterday. She smiled at Flora when she came in, but the expression didn't reach her eyes.

"Did you find your house all right?" Violet asked. As she approached the counter, Flora noticed that her eyes were red and a little puffy, as if she had been crying.

"I did," she said. "And I even managed to find my way back to town without using my GPS. You were right, it's almost a straight shot from here to my house."

Violet chuckled. "Warbler's not complicated. You'll get used to the area in no time. What can I get you today?"

"The same thing I had yesterday. I think it was the…" She looked the menu over, trying to remember what she had ordered.

"The white chocolate caramel latte?" Violet said. She chuckled at Flora's surprised expression. "I think I've got half the town's orders memorized. What's one more? It will be just a second."

Flora paid, then stepped back to wait while Violet made her latte. She was surprised when, halfway through, the woman groaned and threw the entire cup into the trash. "Sorry," she called out to Flora. "Today hasn't been a great day. I started making the wrong drink. It'll be just another second."

"No problem," Flora said. She hesitated, examining the other woman's face. She was smiling, but it looked shaky, and Flora had a suspicion she was just barely holding on to her customer service facade. "I don't mean to be nosy, but are you alright? I know I'm a stranger, but sometimes talking to a stranger helps."

Violet breathed out slowly. "I just got the news this morning that my ex passed away yesterday. We had a … complicated relationship, but it was still such a shock, you know? One day he was there, and the next … he's just gone. I can't help but feel it was my fault. He asked me for a ride, but I was too busy. If I'd gone to get him, he might still be here."

Flora felt a sinking sensation in her stomach. "Was his name Troy, by any chance?"

Violet gasped and stared at her with wide eyes. "How did you know?"

She bit her lip, not sure that this was the best conversation to be having with the grieving woman, but feeling like it was too late to back out now. "I'm the one who found him."

"Oh." Her hand shaking, Violet put down the cup she was holding. "Well. Small world, huh? Would you mind … telling me what happened?"

It wasn't what Flora had expected her to ask, but

she didn't see how she could possibly turn the other woman down. "Okay," she said. "What do you know so far?"

"Just what the police told me," Violet said as she began remaking Flora's drink. "He was the victim of a hit and run. They think he died on impact, and they don't think anyone witnessed it. They brought me in for questioning because they found out he had texted me right before he died, so I'm guessing they don't have any real suspects if I was their best bet."

"Unfortunately, I can't really tell you much more than what you know already," Flora said. "I was driving home from the hardware store just before the storm hit when I saw something on the side of the road. I stopped my truck and got out, and as soon as I realized what had happened, I called the police." She hesitated, not sure if she should mention she had been with Grady or not. She decided not to. In a town this small, she was sure whatever she said would spread, and she didn't want the rumor to somehow mutate and Grady take the blame for it. So far, he had been nothing but nice and helpful to her, and she didn't want to inadvertently mess things up for him more than she already had.

"I just can't believe someone would hit him and then leave him there," Violet said, her voice shaking.

"I'd rather believe they didn't see him, somehow, and thought they just clipped an animal. Because if someone knew they hit a person with their car, you'd think they would stop. But then, a part of me wonders if they hit him on purpose."

"Why would someone do that?" Flora asked. She knew why Officer Hendricks thought *Grady* hit him, but he was the one person she knew for a fact hadn't done it. Had Troy made more enemies in town?

"He had some enemies," Violet said. "He was … ambitious. It's one of the reasons I broke up with him. I'd be lying if I said he didn't nearly drive *me* to murder sometimes, but I'd rather believe that whatever happened was an accident." She sighed. "Thanks for talking to me. I'll be all right, it's just so surprising, you know? I shouldn't be putting all of this on you, though. Tell me about your house. Do you like it here so far?"

"It's been a crazy couple of days, but I think I'm going to really enjoy it here," Flora said. She accepted her cup of coffee from the other woman. "My roof leaks, which was a nasty surprise. It's patched with a tarp for now, but I need to find a company who can redo the whole thing."

"If you're looking for someone local to do it, my uncle, Gordon Hatfield, is the way to go. He's the one who was here when you stopped in yesterday. He owns Hatfield Contracting, and they're right here in town."

"Really?" Flora asked. "Grady—this guy I met at the hardware store—" She hadn't meant to let his name slip out. "Said something about him over-charging."

"No, it's just that Grady undercharges," Violet said. "He thinks anyone who charges a fair price overcharges. Gordon's well known in the area and has a big company, and he works with a lot of different subcontractors. You can stop right in at the office and talk to him, and if you mention I sent you, he might even give you a deal."

Well, it was a two to one vote for Gordon, and Flora really wanted to get her roof fixed. "Thanks. I think I'll do that. I hope things get better for you, and I'm sorry for your loss."

"Thanks," Violet said, a small but real smile on her face. "I'll see you around. Good luck with your house!"

CHAPTER NINE

Flora left with her latte in her hand and the hope that she might be on her way to making a friend. Sure, an understandably upset friend who might have only wanted to talk to her because she knew what happened to her ex-boyfriend, but still. She intended to become a regular at the coffee shop. Even if she and Violet didn't end up clicking, being a regular and known sight around town was bound to help her make some friends. One of the few things she hadn't been prepared for was how socially isolated she felt. Everyone she'd met so far had been nice enough, but it was strange to think that if she wanted to have an evening out, there wasn't anyone she could call up and invite to go with her.

She would get there, she knew. She had always

been a social person who made friends easily, and so what if this was a different world entirely than Chicago had been? People were just people, wherever they were.

She would have to get used to the sense of everyone knowing everyone, though. There were no strangers in town. Or rather, *she* was the only stranger in town. She hoped she wouldn't feel like an outsider forever, but at the same time, she was planning on leaving in two years. Maybe she should try to keep a *little* distance, so she wouldn't be too sad when the time came to leave.

And if she wanted to have a hope of actually flipping this house and buying another one in two years, she needed to focus. She sat in her truck and looked up Hatfield Contracting. The website told her they did all sorts of things—roofing, plumbing, electrical work… If they were any good, she had a feeling she would be working with them a lot. The only thing that made her hesitate to call them was Grady's warning. But Officer Hendricks and Violet had both spoken highly of the company. Two to one seemed like good odds to her, but so far, Grady hadn't steered her wrong, so she wasn't sure what to do. Maybe it would be better to stop by in person like Violet had suggested. She was better at gauging people's personalities face-to-face instead of over the phone.

She typed the company's address into her GPS and pulled away from the curb. It was a nice day, so she kept her windows rolled down as she drove through town. She passed by the grocery store, which she would have to circle back around to, then drove past the police station. She wondered if they had made any progress on Troy's case yet. Probably not. It had only been a day, and she knew police work was much slower in real life than it was on TV.

Hatfield Contracting was only a couple minutes' drive outside of town. It had a nice, paved parking lot and looked customer friendly—a lot more so than she had imagined. She parked and went into the building. The office was small, but it was clean and tidy. It was also empty. She walked up to the front desk, but there was no bell and no information about where she might find someone to help her.

After waiting for a second, she walked over to the window to peer out of it, wondering if she was supposed to go find someone or just wait. She really hoped this company would be able to work with her and get her roof fixed sooner rather than later. She had no idea what a normal wait time for something like replacing a roof was. Weeks? Months? The tarp looked like it would hold for a while, but it wouldn't last forever.

As she looked around for anyone who might be an employee, a white cargo van pulled into the lot and parked a few spaces down from her truck. A middle-aged man got out, slamming the driver's side door behind him. He strode into the office, shoving the door open with enough force that Flora could practically feel the anger radiating off of him. His jaw was clenched, and he looked like he wanted to hit something.

As soon as he spotted her, however, the expression on his face turned into a smile similar to the one the car salesman who had sold her the truck had worn.

"Good afternoon. Have you been helped?"

She shook her head. "No. I just got here. I was hoping to talk to somebody about getting my roof redone."

He nodded and looked around the room, as if hoping a secretary would pop up from behind the desk. A fleeting expression of annoyance crossed his face. "Sorry about your wait. Lola must be on her break. We don't get a lot of walk-in customers. Take a seat, and I'll be with you in a moment."

He disappeared into the back but returned after just a few seconds, a clipboard in his hands. "All right, I'll need your name and your address. I can send someone out in the next couple of days to take a look at the roof and give you a free estimate."

"First, I was wondering what sort of timeline I'd be looking at," Flora said. "I have no idea what to expect. I've never owned a house before."

"Depends," the man said. "We've got a few projects going on right now. Are you local?"

She nodded. "I live a couple miles outside of town. I just bought the house and moved in yesterday. I didn't realize the roof was leaking until I got there. Someone helped me patch it with a tarp, but I know that's only temporary, and I don't think there's any reason to put off fixing it properly."

"Who helped you with the patch?" he asked, making a note on the clipboard.

"A guy I met at the hardware store," she said, not wanting to be too specific. She had to remind herself again that Warbler was tiny, and everyone knew everyone. Even her attempted vagueness didn't seem to work, because the man rolled his eyes as if he knew who she was talking about.

"All right, well, I'm glad you're coming to us instead of trying to scrape the bottom of the barrel for the cheapest work possible. How did you find out about us?"

"Two people recommended you to me," she said. "Officer Hendricks and your niece, Violet. I just came from the coffee shop, actually. I think I saw you there yesterday."

"Oh, right. I thought you looked familiar." He put the clipboard down and shook her hand. "I'm Gordon Hatfield, and I own this place. My niece did the right thing by sending you to me. I'd be happy to slip your roof in between some other projects, and I'll even give you the family and friends discount, since Violet sent you my way."

"Really? Thanks," Flora said, feeling relieved.

"I can come out and look at your roof as soon as Friday," he offered. "We could get started in the next week or two. But since this is a rush project, I'll need you to put down a deposit on the project in order to hold your spot. I can get the papers ready for you to sign in just a couple of minutes."

"Oh." He was moving fast, but this was what she wanted, wasn't it? Having the roof fixed in a matter of weeks would be a huge weight off her shoulders. "Sure. I'll put down a deposit."

He started typing on the computer, and she heard the old printer across the room hum to life. Suddenly, he looked over her shoulder and out the window, a frown flashing across his face. She followed his gaze. A police cruiser was pulling into the parking lot.

"Actually, it looks like I have a meeting I need to take," he said brusquely. "If you give me your email address, I'll send you the contract. I'll accept the deposit when I come to look at your roof. Friday works? Eleven?"

She was a little thrown by how suddenly everything had changed, but she nodded. "Yeah." At least it would give her more time to think this through. "That sounds good. I'll keep an eye out for the email."

She shook his hand again and turned toward the door just as Officer Hendricks walked inside. He recognized her—she could tell by how his eyebrows rose in surprise—but didn't comment. He simply held the door for her as she exited the office. She glanced back over her shoulder, wondering what he was doing here, and if it had anything to do with Troy. According to Officer Hendricks, Troy used to work for Gordon, right?

She shook her head and continued to her truck. Troy's case had nothing to do with her. What mattered was that she was going to get her roof fixed, and in record time too. She tried to focus on the positives as she headed back into town to *finally* do her grocery shopping.

CHAPTER TEN

Flora felt much better with her fridge—and her stomach—full. The little grocery store didn't have all the options she was used to, but it had enough that she could get the basics and make a good dinner. After she ate, she cleaned, focusing on sweeping the floors and washing the counters in the kitchen and bathroom for now. She only got the first floor done, but it felt good to have everything a little less dusty and to be sure that there was no rat poison lying around. She shut the doors to the upstairs rooms to keep Amaretto out, then let the cat out of the office so she could start to explore the house.

As the sun began to fall, she grabbed the flashlight she had picked up at the store and tucked the box of lightbulbs under her elbow before she opened the basement door. She really wanted to be able to do laundry, so it was time to explore the basement. She stepped down onto the first step and shut the basement door behind her so Amaretto couldn't follow her. She immediately regretted it. She enjoyed watching horror movies, but suddenly, she wished she hadn't watched quite so many slasher flicks over the years. The basement was *creepy.* The stairs were ancient and warped, and she couldn't see anything but the dark, cracked concrete floor at the bottom of them. It looked wan and too stark in the illumination from the flashlight. She told herself she was being silly, but as soon as she reached the bottom of the stairs, she spun in a quick circle, checking every corner of the room with the beam of light.

The basement was empty. Of course it was—what else had she expected? There was a furnace and a water heater, both of which looked old but probably functional. On the opposite side of the basement were the washer and dryer. They were a lot older than the models she was used to in her old apartment, but the listing had claimed they worked, and she was going to believe it until she discovered otherwise.

She looked around until she found where the single lightbulb was hanging from the low ceiling and replaced it with a new one, then returned to the top of the stairs to flick the switch. The warm glow that lit up the basement was much better than her flashlight, and as Flora walked back down the stairs, she tried to figure out what she wanted to do to the place. With some paint, the floor and the walls wouldn't be that bad, and then maybe whoever moved in when she sold the house could use this space as an exercise room, or even a hangout space if they had older kids.

She could decide later. For now, she had laundry to do, and the house to continue working on.

Flora's to-do list only continued to grow as the evening went on. She spent half the night looking at cheap furniture online, and finally broke down and ordered a mattress from an online store that promised to deliver it by Saturday. The mattress was one thing she didn't want to buy used, and she didn't want to sleep on the floor for longer than she had to. She ignored the urge to go crazy buying new decor for her house and focused on what she actually needed. She had spotted a couple of secondhand stores in town, and she started making a list for what she wanted to get there. A kitchen table and chairs, a coat rack, somewhere to put her shoes when she came in, and definitely some rugs. The house's wooden floors were dry and scraped up, and she had a bad feeling she would regret every single piece of dirt she tracked in when the time to refinish the floors came. The list of things she had to do *around* the house kept growing too, and that was just to make it livable while she worked on actually renovating it.

She decided to swing by the hardware store again tomorrow to pick up some of what she wanted and went to bed with her mind swirling with thoughts of what she was going to do the next day.

When she drove into town the next morning, she slowed at the spot where she had found Troy's body. She wondered if she would always do that, if the memory of that afternoon would ever leave her. It seemed wrong to just ignore what had happened, so she paused briefly and sent a silent apology to the man who had died, then continued on into town.

She headed straight to the hardware store, parking out front along the curb like she had before. She was armed with a list this time and knew exactly what she needed for her first few projects. It had been embarrassing to go in so underprepared the first time, and she didn't want to repeat the experience.

The old man wasn't behind the register when she went in, but other than that, the hardware store looked exactly the same as it had before. She hadn't thought to check and see if Grady's truck was parked in the back lot, but she figured if he wasn't here, whoever *was* could tell her when he would be in. Maybe they could pass a message to him. She remembered he had said he didn't have a cell phone, but he had offered to help her with other projects, so he probably had a way to be contacted—maybe a landline? She grabbed a cart and pushed it back toward where she remembered seeing the paint. Since she was just getting white, she didn't need anyone to mix it for her. She spent far too long gazing at the different cans and trying to decide what she wanted. In the end, she ended up going with a high gloss white paint, since gloss was supposed to be easier to clean and she didn't want to have to redo all of her hard work in two years. It was just for the trim throughout the house, but it would be an easy and satisfying project to work on whenever she wasn't in the mood to tackle something harder.

She grabbed a multi pack of paintbrushes and a plastic tarp, then wandered around looking for the sandpaper. She was walking past the tarps when Grady came in through the door to the outdoor lot.

"Grady," she called out. "Hi."

He looked surprised to see her. "Hey," he said. "How's your roof holding up?"

"Well, the tarp's still up there, so it seems to be doing pretty well. I guess the real test will be when it rains again. But someone's coming out tomorrow to give me an estimate on getting the whole roof redone. They said they could probably fit me in sometime in the next couple of weeks."

"That's good," he said. "Who did you end up going with?"

She hesitated. "Well, Gordon Hatfield. Someone else I know recommended him, and so did that police officer I talked to. I met him, and he seems all right." She remembered how she felt like he had been rushing her, but she pushed the concerns away. She hadn't received the email he had promised to send, so she hadn't signed anything yet. She could still change her mind.

Grady frowned. "Well, I hope you're happy with his work."

"I'm sure it'll be fine. I know you don't like him very much, but he can't be that bad."

Grady gave her a skeptical look but didn't say anything.

She plunged onward. "Anyway, I do have some other projects I need help with. You mentioned you're kind of a handyman, right? Well, I'd like to try to fix the ceiling where the roof was leaking. I might also need some help getting some furniture into my house. I'd be happy to pay you, of course."

"I can help," he said. "When are you getting the furniture?"

"Today, hopefully. I'm going to check the thrift stores to see what's available." It didn't make much sense to buy completely new stuff when she was just going to be moving again in a few years.

"I can come out tomorrow," he offered. "Would that work?"

She grinned. "Perfect. Thank you. I should be home all day, so just come by whenever. Oh, and I'll give you my number in case you need to reschedule."

She wrote her number out for him at the register, and learned he did have a landline—which she, in turn, got the number to. When she left the hardware store, she felt like she had accomplished something. It was a good feeling, one she wanted to hold on to.

Now, it was time to go furniture shopping and hope everything she wanted to buy could fit in the bed of her truck.

CHAPTER ELEVEN

Flora spent that evening sitting on her porch in the camp chair, sipping some hot tea. Her stops at the thrift stores in town had netted her a small kitchen table and chair set, along with various, currently deconstructed bed frames, and even a couch. She had managed to move the bed frames inside, but the couch was still in the back of her truck. She'd been quite grateful for those ratchet straps Grady had encouraged her to buy a couple of days ago when the employees had helped her load everything up. The weather app on her phone claimed it wasn't supposed to rain tonight, which was good, because she wouldn't be able to get the couch inside until she had help.

Other than the warm glow of the porch light by

the door, the only lights Flora could see were the stars. It was beautiful out here, and silent other than for the crickets and frogs. She could see herself doing this every night, sitting out on the porch with a warm drink and Amaretto perched just on the other side of the screen in the open living room window, keeping her company in her aloof, catlike way. Her arms were smudged with paint, and she was tired, but … today had been a good day. She'd been busy, and it had been hard work to carry most of the furniture inside herself and spend hours scrubbing the sinks and bathtub with cleaning chemicals, but it felt satisfying in a way she hadn't experienced for a long time.

And tomorrow, Gordon was going to come over, and she would finally know how much her roof repair was going to cost. She wasn't looking forward to spending the money, but she was sure she would make it back when the time came to sell the house. A new roof would be a big draw, right? She had to start thinking long-term with her money. Cutting corners wouldn't do her any favors in the end.

She woke with a crick in her neck the next morning. Her cat was meowing imperiously at the bedroom door, demanding to be let out of the small makeshift bedroom. Amaretto had trained her well, because Flora fed her breakfast before she got ready for the day. She made extra coffee, just in case Grady wanted some whenever he came over, and she fried herself some eggs at the stove before sitting at her new-to-her table to enjoy her first real breakfast in her house.

After she was done with her coffee and eggs, she grabbed her painting supplies and started working on the trim in the hallway. It was slow going, since she had to sand the old paint off the wood first. A few minutes before eleven, she heard tires on gravel and looked out the window to see Gordon Hatfield's white van pulling up behind her truck.

Pausing to replace the lid on the paint can so Amaretto couldn't somehow get covered in the stuff, she slipped her shoes on and stepped outside. Gordon slammed his van door shut and greeted her with a nod, before looking up at her roof.

"I'm going to need to go up there," he said, opening the back of his van to pull a ladder similar to the one she owned out. "This will take a few minutes. I've got to check the condition of your shingles, figure out how many layers there are, and take some measurements of the pitch of the roof. Do you have anywhere to be?"

She shook her head. "I'll be here all day; I'm just working on painting inside. Do you want some coffee?"

He shook his head wordlessly and carried his ladder over to the house, leaning it against the roof near the open living room window. He didn't seem to be in a talkative mood, which was fine by her. He didn't need to be her best friend, he just needed to fix her roof for a fair price, and she would be happy.

She went back inside and sat down to continue painting but only just picked up her brush when she heard the sound of someone else pulling into her driveway. This time, she bounded up a little more excitedly. It was probably Grady, though he hadn't given her an exact time he would be there. He might not exactly be a chatterbox himself, but at least he was a friendly face. She wondered if this lack of social interaction was slowly driving her insane—and it had only been a few days. She would start being a crazy cat lady in earnest if she didn't make some friends soon.

Sure enough, his truck with its dented grille was parked behind Gordon's van. Flora stepped back out onto the porch, hearing Gordon's footsteps as he walked across the roof above her.

"Hey!" she called, waving to Grady, who was already getting out of his truck. He nodded at her but turned his attention to Gordon on the roof immediately after, a furrow in his brow, and she wondered if this was a bad idea.

"Can you help me with the couch?" she asked, pointing to her truck. Grady tore his eyes away from Gordon and nodded again, striding over to begin undoing the ratchets that had held the couch in the bed of the truck while she drove. She walked over to help him.

"Thanks for coming out," she said. "I really appreciate it."

"It's no problem," he said quietly. "Did that guy give you a price yet?"

She shook her head. "Not yet. He needs to … measure, and stuff, I guess."

"You should get a couple quotes, at least," he said. "See for yourself if he's offering you a fair deal."

She shrugged, not sure if she appreciated his advice or not. On the one hand, if Gordon really was known for overcharging, it was nice of Grady to warn her away. On the other hand, if he just had personal issues with the man, she wished he would let it drop.

As Grady pulled the ratchet straps away, Flora realized she should probably put Amaretto in the other room so she could leave the front door open without worrying about her running out. She told Grady she would be right back and returned to her house, finding Amaretto gazing out the open living room window. She carried her to the office, popped her down on the cat bed, and shut the door firmly behind her.

"I'll let you out soon," she promised from the other side of it. The cat didn't like being locked in anywhere, and she felt bad as she walked away to the sound of pitiful meows.

She left the front door open when she went back outside, hoping the couch would fit through it. Grady was waiting for her by the truck. He hopped up into the bed and lifted the far end of the couch, while she lifted the end that was closest to her. The couch was heavy, but they managed to move it until the back foot or so of it was resting on the truck's tailgate. They rested it there while Grady jumped down out of the truck bed and oriented himself to lift it from the ground. Flora only made it a few steps before she had to lower her end down and take a break.

"Sorry," she said, wiggling her fingers in an effort to get blood flowing back into them. "I'm going to need to start working out. This is heavy."

She bent down to pick up the couch again and found herself eye-level with the front of Gordon's van. Something about it seemed off. It took her a second to realize that the bumper was zip-tied on, and it was a slightly different shade of white than the rest of the van, as if it had been taken from another vehicle. And right there, under the lip of the van's hood, was a dark, rusty red smudge.

Flora felt like she had just jumped out of an airplane, though she hadn't moved a step. She had seen a white van on her way into town, just half an hour before they found Troy's body. It hadn't stood out to her at the time, because vans like this were everywhere, and she hadn't known yet that she would find the victim of a fatal hit-and-run accident on her way back home. But now, it did stand out to her, because hadn't Troy used to work for Gordon, before he stole a list of customers and branched out on his own? That smudge … it looked suspiciously like blood. And the bumper … it looked like it might have belonged to another vehicle not too long ago, before being hastily put on this one.

Gordon's bad attitude and the nervous look on his face when the police officer stopped by the office flashed through her mind.

She realized belatedly that she had frozen in place and Grady was staring at her in concern. She needed to tell him about this, but not out here. Not with Gordon still up on her roof. She didn't dare look over to see if the other man was watching them, for fear he would see something on her face. She could only hope he hadn't seen her staring at his van. Trying to act normal, she bent down and picked up her half of the couch again.

She barely noticed how her muscles burned as they moved it toward her house. Her heart was pounding too fast, and her mind was racing.

Either she was going crazy, or Gordon Hatfield was the one who killed Troy.

CHAPTER TWELVE

They had to rotate the couch around a few times to figure out how to fit it through the door, but they made it without causing too much damage to anything. Grady frowned and rubbed at one of the minor scrape marks on the door, but Flora wasn't concerned. The damage to her house was the last thing on her mind.

They carried the couch into the living room and set it down near the window, then Flora pressed her finger to her lips and crept back over to the door to close it quietly. Then, she turned to her companion and said, "I'm pretty sure I have a murderer on my roof."

Grady, who had been looking around the interior

of her house with curiosity, inhaled sharply enough that he coughed. "What?"

"I forgot until now, but … on my way to the hardware store the day we found Troy, I saw a white van coming from town. I didn't pay any attention to it of course—I didn't have any reason to think it would be important at the time. But now I'm pretty sure it was Gordon's van. I had seen him at the coffee shop not long before that." She dragged a hand through her hair and sat down heavily on the couch. It smelled like old people, and she vaguely wished she had thought to buy some fabric freshener spray. "The bumper on his van is zip tied on," she explained. "When I bent down to pick up the couch, I realized the color is a little off, and there's a smear of something that looks like blood just under the lip of the hood. I don't know—maybe he hit a deer a few weeks ago or maybe it's just mud or oil, but … it makes sense, Grady. Don't you see? Troy used to work for him, right?"

He nodded slowly. "It was a big deal around town for a couple weeks. He quit at Hatfield Contracting and took the client list with him, then went around undercutting their prices and offering to do his own work. It was talked about a lot, because people suspected he had set the move up years ago. He was dating Gordon's niece, see, who got him an in with the company. I heard someone had to call the police on Gordon at some point for threatening Troy. That was about six months ago."

"I just realized, he knew where Troy was going to be," Flora said, her eyes widening. "When I stopped at the coffee shop that day, he was there talking to Violet, his niece. She got a text, and I remember her mentioning it was her ex, asking for a ride because his car had broken down on his way home from a friend's house. She couldn't go get him because she was at work, but Gordon *knew* he would be walking down that road."

"What do we do?" Grady asked. "I believe you, but we don't have proof."

"I don't know. Call the police, I guess? The blood on his van might be enough. Even if it isn't, I'd rather have them *here*. I don't trust him, even if he doesn't know we know."

She stood up, intending to go find her phone, when she heard a sound that made her blood run cold. The creak of someone standing on her front porch.

Slowly, her eyes moved to the living room window. It was open. Of course it was open. She'd left it open, because Amaretto liked sitting on the sill and looking out. And right next to the window was where Gordon's ladder was leaning. If he had heard them talking, if he had come down quietly and overheard everything they said…

She stared at her front door, trying to remember if she had locked it or not. Grady shifted, peering out the window and toward the porch, then all of a sudden, he lunged forward and grabbed her by the arm, pulling her toward him.

Before she could struggle, he whispered in her ear, "He's standing on the porch, and he has a gun."

Her blood ran cold. He must have heard them. She was shocked, at first, that he had been carrying a gun on his person, then realized that this was a very different world from the city she was used to. In a small town like this, nestled in rural Kentucky, guns were probably as common as coffee machines.

"We need to get out of here," he whispered.

She nodded, but then froze again. "Amaretto."

He looked at her like she was crazy, and she realized she hadn't mentioned her cat to him, so the word probably seemed nonsensical. Now wasn't the time for a discussion, though. She just nodded at the office door, and they started moving toward it in the same instant she heard Gordon knock at the front door. She gulped, and pushed the office door open, stooping automatically to grab the fluffy white cat before she could run out.

Grady gave the cat a glance, then moved past her to the office window. He popped the screen out, and Flora carefully shut the office door behind her before following him over to it. She could hear Gordon shouting her name and pounding at the front door as Grady slipped outside and held out his arms for the cat.

Thankfully, Amaretto didn't struggle as Flora handed her over. As soon as the cat was outside, she followed, scraping her arm a little on the window frame as she went out. Grady handed the cat back to her, then silently reached up to pull the window shut.

They were out of the house, and Gordon had no idea where they were. That was good.

Then, she heard a crash that she guessed was the other man kicking in the front door. That was less good. Her heart in her throat, she exchanged a wide-eyed look with Grady. Keeping low and close to the house, so he wouldn't be able to see them out the window unless he looked straight down, they crept around to the front. Sure enough, the front door was open, and Gordon was nowhere to be seen.

"My keys are still inside," she whispered, peering around the corner to where her truck was.

"Mine are in my truck," he whispered back. "We should make a run for it."

She took a deep breath, and as soon as she made sure they were on the same wavelength, they darted out around the side of the house, past the front door, and then ducked around to the other side of Grady's truck. They crouched behind it and listened, but she didn't hear any footsteps or any other indication Gordon had heard them.

"He's going to hear us start the truck," she murmured to Grady. "What if he follows us in his van?"

"He probably left the keys in it," he whispered. "We could take them."

Flora clutched Amaretto to her chest, thinking. Then, she shoved the cat at Grady. "Take her and get in your truck. I'll check his van for the keys. Be ready to go as soon as I'm done."

Before he could argue, she hurried over to the van, keeping it between her and the house. Both of the windows were down, and it was a simple matter to lean in and snatch the keys out of the cupholder. She was about to dart back to Grady's truck when Gordon's cell phone, which was sitting right in front of her nose on the dashboard, started to ring.

It would be good to have a phone to call the police

with, and since hers was inside and Grady didn't have one, Gordon's would do nicely. She snatched it off the dashboard and ran back to the truck, throwing caution to the wind. She yanked the passenger side door open and slid in next to Grady, who shoved the cat into her lap and cranked the engine. The truck roared to life, and he slammed it into reverse. They swung out onto the road. Flora heard a sharp crack, and the truck's back window shattered. She turned to see Gordon aiming the gun at them from just inside her front door, but they were already far enough away he didn't try for a second shot. He ran for his van, and she fought back a surge of giddiness. They had done it. They had made it out with their lives—and, unless he had a spare key, he wouldn't be able to follow them.

In her hand, his phone started ringing again. Violet's name came up on the screen. Flora blinked at it, then, more out of habit than anything, she answered the call.

"Hello?"

"Uncle—" Violet started, then paused. "Who is this?"

"It's Flora." She felt stunned, as if a large part of her was unable to believe she had just been *shot* at. She knew she should hang up and call the police, but Violet's next words stopped her.

"I have no idea why you're answering my uncle's phone, but the police are at my coffee shop, and they're looking for him. Can you put him on? They … they say they have a warrant for his arrest."

"Sorry," Flora said, glancing over at Grady. He looked just as stunned as she felt, but he still had the presence of mind to raise an eyebrow, silently asking her what in the world she was doing. "I can't do that. He just tried to kill me, and we're running away. Did you say the police are there? Could I talk to them?"

"He tried to—Flora, what's going *on?* Hold on, I'm handing the phone over."

She heard the sound of someone fumbling the phone, then heard Officer Hendrick's voice on the other line. She took in a shuddering breath and started to explain exactly what had happened—and where they could find the man they were looking for.

EPILOGUE

Thunder rumbled loud enough to make the windows shake, and rain pelted down outside. Flora was standing in the second-floor bedroom, gazing up at the ceiling, a smile on her face. No drips. This was the first heavy rain since she and Grady had installed the tarp, and it was working. Relief took a weight off her shoulders. The tarp might not be a *permanent* solution, but sometimes a stopgap measure would do just fine.

Satisfied that she wasn't going to wake up to a puddle of water on the floor in the morning, she went back downstairs, where Amaretto was waiting for her on the couch, her fluffy white form curled up in a pile of blankets. Somehow, the cat had claimed *all* the blankets, while Flora had none, but she didn't have the heart to disturb the spoiled cat's rest. She sat down at the other end of the couch and leaned forward to press play on her laptop. It was the perfect night for a horror movie.

As she settled back against the cushions, her phone buzzed, and she leaned forward to pick it up. It was a text message from Violet.

Are you free tomorrow?

Flora smiled as she typed out her response. *Grady's coming over to help me replace my front door, but I'm free other than that.*

You should meet me and my friends for lunch, came the quick reply. *It'll be fun.*

She typed out a response, accepting the invitation instantly. She had thought Violet would be upset at her involvement with her uncle's arrest, but when she finally got up the courage to stop by the coffee shop again the next week, the other woman had been the one apologizing to *her.* Violet might have seemed prickly the first time Flora met her, but her second impression had been the right one. Violet was quickly becoming her first friend here in Warbler … or, maybe her second one. Grady still hadn't let her pay him for any of his help, and he had come out twice more to help her with things she had mentioned in passing. Flora had taken to stopping at both the coffee shop and the hardware store almost every time she went into town. They were two very different people, but somehow, they both made her feel welcome here.

Warbler, Kentucky was nothing like what she was used to, and Flora was beginning to realize that was exactly what she needed.

Printed in Great Britain
by Amazon

27340091R00067